For Ron Maurer, Andi Manpearl, Richard Ross,
and Barbara Bottner—four amazing teachers
who encouraged me to tell stories.

An imprint of Astra Books for Young Readers,
a division of Astra Publishing House
astrapublishinghouse.com
Printed in China

ISBN: 978-1-6626-4016-2 (hc)
ISBN: 978-1-6626-4017-9 (eBook)
Library of Congress Control Number: 2022901201

First edition
10 9 8 7 6 5 4 3 2 1

Design by Amelia Mack
The text is set in Quincy.
The illustrations are done digitally.

A DELICIOUS Story

Barney Saltzberg

Hippo Park

Hello!

What are you doing here?!

I'm looking for
a story.

Oh . . .
I haven't seen one.

Wait, isn't this a book?

Yes, this *is* a book . . .
but there's no story.

How is that possible?

I don't want to talk about it.

What happend to the story?

There were pictures, too.

There was a story and pictures?

It had everything—
a beginning, a middle,
and an end.

Where did everything go?

Don't you think it's nice and peaceful here?

It's okay, but it would be much better with a story.

Stop and listen. Isn't the quiet refreshing?

Uh . . . I suppose.

So why would we need anything else?

WAIT A MINUTE!
You're trying to trick me.
What happened to
the story?

I couldn't help myself.
I was hungry.

You ate the story?
And the pictures?

Yes, and *what a* delicious story it was.

Maybe I can make up a new one for you?

I would like that.

Give me a minute to think.

Okay.

How's it going?

I'm not so sure.

I didn't know it was
so hard to make up
a story.

WELL IT IS...

WHEN YOU'RE STARING AT ME!

How do you expect me to make up a story while you watch?

Well, if you hadn't eaten the story you wouldn't *have* to make up a new one!

I have an idea!

I need to be ALONE
when I create!

ALONE!
By myself.

Now I don't have
a story and I don't
have you.

WAIT!
That's it!

Once there was a little mouse who was looking for a story...

But a big mouse had eaten it all up. So there was no story to be found.

And even though the little mouse didn't find a story, he did make a new friend. The end.

That is a story,
but I don't want it
to end there.

Where do you want it to end?

I like surprise
endings.

THAT was a surprise ending!

To a great story!

Can we hear it again?

Once there was a little mouse and a dragon who were looking for...

a delicious story...

with a **SURPRISE** ending!

Yes, but we can read it again.

Is that the end of the book?